Spray, the Bug

The Importance of Commas

By Joyce Shui
Illustrated by James Smith

Archway Publishing books may be ordered through booksellers or by contacting:

Archway Publishing
1663 Liberty Drive
Bloomington, IN 47403
www.archwaypublishing.com
844-669-3957

Authored by Joyce Shui
Inspired by Lima Xu
Illustrated by James Smith
With thanks to The Purple School®

Interior Image Credit: James Smith

ISBN: 978-1-6657-5218-3 (sc)
ISBN: 978-1-6657 5219-0 (e)

Library of Congress Control Number: 2023920514

Print information available on the last page.

Archway Publishing rev. date: 11/30/2023

ARCHWAY
PUBLISHING

Once upon a time, there was a bug named "Spray." Everything was fine for a while. Spray lived a happy life with loving, doting parents. And he was excited to start kindergarten.

Then he started kindergarten.

His teacher introduced Spray on the first day, "Hello, class. This is . . . Spray the bug."

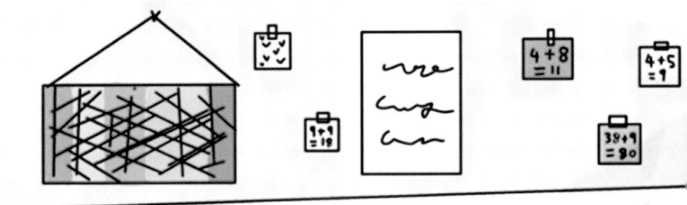

Suddenly, several of Spray's classmates,

Kiki, the cat,
Huiling, the horse, and
Daichi, the dog,

rushed at Spray.

Kiki, the cat, sprayed Spray with perfume.

Daichi, the dog, sprayed Spray with a water bottle.

And Huiling, the horse, sprayed Spray with a can of non-toxic foam.

The teacher looked at the other kids and at Spray, the bug, in disbelief and confusion.

Spray, the bug, was wet and also very confused.

"Oh, my dear," Spray's teacher then realized. "I needed to use a comma! Kids, this is Spray, the bug. His *name* is Spray. Please do not spray Spray, the bug."

"Oh," said the kids. "We're really sorry."

At recess, the kids all happily dashed to the playground. Huiling, the horse, was excited to introduce Spray, the bug, to one of her friends from another class.

"This is Spray the bug," she said to Soso, the salamander.

In the blink of an eye, Soso, the salamander, squirted Spray with a can of olive oil spray she carried everywhere.

"Oh, my," Huiling, the horse, said. "Our teacher just told us about the importance of commas. I should've told you that this is my new friend, Spray, the bug, not to spray the bug."

"Oh," said Soso, the salamander. "Deep apologies."

At lunch, Soso and Spray, the bug, sat next to each other. Soso introduced Spray to another new friend, Lima, the lion. "Lima, this is . . . Spray the bug."

Lima, the lion, sprayed Spray with a barrage of salt.

"Oh, my," exclaimed Soso, the salamander. "Huiling told me about the importance of commas. Lima, this is my friend, Spray, the bug. Please do not spray Spray, the bug."

"Oh, I beg your pardon. I'm very sorry. It's nice to meet you, Spray," said Lima, the lion.

In the afternoon, all the little kids sat for circle time. They introduced themselves. When it was Spray's turn, he very carefully used a comma, "Hello. I'm Spray, the bug." Then he braced himself.

"Hello, Spray, the bug!" the teacher and all the kindergartners cheered with very careful, intentional use of the comma!

Spray was dry and so very happy to make new friends who now knew the importance of commas.

When Spray got home from school that afternoon, his father asked him, "How was your first day of school?"

"Great!" smiled Spray. He told his parents, "We learned all about commas."

"That's great," his mother said to him, "because I have a surprise. We have new neighbors next door. Their child will start kindergarten tomorrow in your class. Her name is Roast, the chicken."

Questions:

1) When there's been a misunderstanding, what are some good words to use?

2) How many commas are there in the story?

3) How many math errors can you spot in the book?

Answer key:

1) Sorry. Apologies. Pardon. Excuse me.

2) 82. (Hint: look at the illustrations)

3) There are seven math errors.

Page 3: 1+1 = <u>2</u>
Page 4: 4+8 = <u>12</u>
Page 5: 21+3 = <u>24</u>
Page 10: 1+2 = <u>3</u>
Page 15: 8+4 = <u>12</u>
Page 16: 8+9 = <u>17</u>
Page 17: 4+4 = <u>8</u>

Made in United States
North Haven, CT
28 December 2023

46723379R10018